Anne Fine

Genie Genie Genie

Illustrated by David Higham

EGMONT

A Sudden Puff of Glittering Smoke
For Vinit

A Sudden Swirl of Icy Wind
For Mary and William

First published as three separate volumes:
A Sudden Puff of Glittering Smoke
First published in Great Britain 1989
by Piccadilly Press

A Sudden Swirl of Icy Wind
First published in Great Britain 1990
by Piccadilly Press

A Sudden Glow of Gold
First published in Great Britain 1991
by Piccadilly Press

Published in this omnibus edition 2004
by Egmont Books Limited
239 Kensington High Street, London W8 6SA

ISBN 1 4052 1202 0

3 5 7 9 10 8 6 4 2

A CIP catalogue record for this title is available from the British Library

Printed and bound in Great Britain by the CPI Group

A Sudden Puff of Glittering Smoke

CHAPTER ONE

Jeanie sat at her desk, twisting the ring on her finger round and round. The ring was bothering her terribly. It was so tight she couldn't get it off. She'd only found it a couple of hours before, glinting so brightly in the gutter she was astonished no one else had noticed it. She'd picked it up and looked around, wondering what to do. Then, when the school bell rang, she'd pushed it hastily onto a finger and run the last few yards into the playground.

But in her hurry she had shoved it on the wrong finger. Now she'd been struggling with it all through register.

1

"Call out your name if you are having a school dinner today," ordered Mr Piper.

"David!"

"Asha!"

"William!"

"Jeanie!"

As she called out her name, she couldn't help giving the ring another little twist.

There was a sudden puff of glittering smoke, and the ring was spinning on the desk in front of her. Jeanie drew her hand away smartly, and stared in wonder.

Before her eyes, the smoke turned to a column of glistening fog, then formed a spinning ball, then took – slowly, slowly – a strange and ancient shape.

It was a genie.

No doubt about it. He was no taller than her pencil and mist still curled around him; but he looked like every genie she had ever seen in books: a little fat in the belly, with a silk bodice and billowing pantaloons that looked for all the world as if they had been woven from silver shifting mists. Tiny stars winked all over them, and they were held up

2

by a belt of pure gold. On his feet were the tiniest curly slippers, with pointed ends.

Folding his arms, the genie bowed low.

"Greetings," he said.

Jeanie just stared, scarcely believing what she saw. She gave herself a little shake, and looked around the classroom. But nobody else seemed to have noticed this odd little creature standing in a pool of mist on her desk.

Extraordinary!

Was she dreaming? Was it possible? Had some old, old magic come her way?

"Who are you?" she whispered.

"I am the genie of the ring," the small apparition with the folded arms declared. "You called me."

"*I* called you?"

"*Genie*, you called."

"Not G-e-n-i-e! *J-e-a-n-i-e!*"

The creature shrugged.

"One little mistake," he said. "Even a genie gets rusty after five hundred years stuck in a ring."

"Five hundred years!"

4

Jeanie was horrified. She felt sorry enough for herself, stuck in the classroom all day. But five hundred years stuck in a ring!

The genie, however, simply waved a hand, lightly dismissing whole lifetimes left unlived.

"Where Hope is lost, Patience must reign. In the end there will always be someone."

"And it was me! So now you're *mine*."

The genie looked her up and down coolly, and raised his eyebrows. Jeanie blushed. She wished she had taken the trouble that morning to put on something fancier than her plain shirt and faded jeans. To judge from the shimmering finery the genie wore, he had been used to far better days and far richer places.

But it wasn't her clothes he was noticing, but her bad manners.

"You do not *own* me," he corrected her sternly. "I serve the ring. It just so happens you were wearing it."

Now Jeanie blushed even more deeply.

It was the genie's turn to feel sorry for her.

"Put on the ring," he told her more gently.

"It would be such a shame to lose it now."

Obediently Jeanie picked up the ring from where it still lay in a little cloud of vapour. She slipped it on, and it felt chilly to the touch. She chose a better finger for it this time. It fitted more comfortably than before.

The genie looked up at her, towering over him.

"And now," he said. "Your wish is my wish."

"I wish . . . I wish . . ."

She glanced round the classroom. Everyone else had settled down to work, and Mr Piper was standing by Asha's desk, chatting to her. No one had seen, no one had heard a thing. Clearly the genie was invisible to everyone except the person who had rubbed the ring. Even the conversations with him were somehow silent. No one would ever know what she wished.

She could choose anything in the world. But what? Now that the ring was safe on her finger, she would have plenty of time to think up wonderful wishes to last a lifetime. What should she choose right now, stuck in the classroom?

"I'd like a brilliant day."

"A brilliant day?"

"Yes. I want one of those days when everything I say and everything I do makes people stare at me in amazement."

The genie shook his head, and sighed. But he'd been in the business of granting secret wishes for over seven thousand years. He knew a lot about the human soul. He only said:

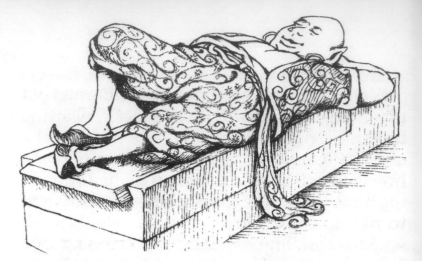

"Your whim is my command."

And then he stretched himself out on the lid of her pencil box, and tucking his hands beneath his head, lay as though sprawled out on golden sands, entirely relaxed, his fat little paunch rising and falling gently with each breath.

Jeanie was a little suspicious. He didn't *look* as if he was organising anything brilliant. But just at that moment Mr Piper began to talk to the class about the fact that it was Asha's last day, she was leaving for India.

"Flying home to the sun," said Mr Piper, waving at the rain beating against the window panes. "Off to a hotter place."

The genie stirred.

"Ah," he murmured. "So many glorious hot places I remember. Arabia. . . Africa. . . India. . ."

"Who can name somewhere else really hot?" asked Mr Piper.

"Where are you from?" Jeanie whispered to the genie.

"Baghdad," he replied, idly crossing one leg over the other and picking at a loose thread in his silver slipper. "It was the shining jewel of all Arabia."

"Baghdad!" called out Jeanie, and added without thinking, "It was the shining jewel of all Arabia."

Mr Piper's eyes widened.

"Well done! And can you tell us anything more about it?"

She glanced down at the genie, still lazing on the desk. Could she?

The genie smiled. Then, gently, he blew. A stream of glittering mist flew up from his mouth and swirled around Jeanie like rings around a planet.

"In the good old days," she heard herself

saying, "Baghdad was truly a city of marvels. Mere words cannot describe its mysteries or its wonders."

Everyone stared. Mr Piper's mouth dropped open. The genie shut his eyes till his dark lashes fluttered on his cheeks, and blew and blew, and Jeanie began to speak of the most magnificent palace from which four highways ran out through massive gateways in high walls, and stretched to the corners of the old Arab empire. She spoke of merchants travelling east and west, and of enormous wealth and terrible poverty. She used words she had never used before – words she had never even heard! She told them about the ruler – Caliph, she called him. She told them about mosques made of finely patterned tiles where Muslims gathered to worship Allah. She spoke of vast bazaars humming with people buying and selling.

"Jeanie!" cried Mr Piper. "You must have spent the whole weekend locked in the library, to know so much!"

Jeanie tried to stop. But the genie still blew. The glittering rings still circled round her head. Without wanting to keep on, she found herself telling Mr Piper all about houses built of sun-dried bricks, white-

11

washed to hurl the heat of the fierce sun back in its face. She told him about cool hidden courtyards and wooden shutters that kept out the sun by day and the desert winds by night.

"Anyone would think you had lived there all your life!"

She wanted the genie to stop blowing. But his eyes were closed. Oh, he was thousands of miles away – and on Jeanie had to go, telling Mr Piper about young boys with dark and shining eyes who drove their donkeys through the narrow streets, selling their firewood or water from leather bags.

"Shall we stop there for a moment?"

Stop? She couldn't stop. Now she was speaking of the riches of Arabia: perfumes, fleet horses, licorice, coffee –

"Jeanie –"

Too late! Already she was praising all the Arabian scholars who had treasured learning, the mathematicians and architects, the doctors and astronomers and philosophers.

"Jeanie!"

Everyone had turned to look at her. She

must stop. But the magic was too powerful. The genie was still blowing.

"No more!" she implored him silently. "Stop!"

"For the love of Allah!" he cried impatiently, opening his eyes at last. "We've only just begun! You haven't even mentioned the wandering Bedouin tribes who live in tents of camel's hair and move through the blinding desert heat from one cool oasis to another!"

"Stop, please!" Jeanie begged the genie.

"Stop, please!" Mr Piper begged Jeanie.

The genie took no notice. He just blew.

"There is a Bedouin curse," Jeanie told her astonished classmates. "It goes: *May God cause you to live in a city*."

"That's really interesting, Jeanie," said Mr Piper. "But – "

Jeanie couldn't help interrupting him.

"They are an honourable people, the Bedouin. Even an enemy is given food and shelter for three days. It is a hard life, though it's lived by choice. They – "

"Jeanie!" cried Mr Piper.

14

"Genie!" cried Jeanie.

The genie sat bolt upright, outraged.

"What about all the rest?" he demanded. "*Salaam*, the daily greeting, *Peace*? The treasures and harems and eunuchs and fabulous carpets? The soaring minarets from which the muezzin call the faithful to prayer? The slaves and snake charmers and –"

Reaching down, Jeanie swatted him off the desk.

He fell in a shower of sparks, turning over and over in shimmering somersaults until he reached the floor, silent at last.

There, glowering at Jeanie from between narrowed eyes, he spun round and round on the curled tip of one of his embroidered slippers. Faster he spun – until his features were blurred. *Faster* – until he had become a

glowing ball. *Faster and faster still* – until he was a spinning column of glistening fog.

Then – *puff! flash!* He was gone.

For just a moment Jeanie felt the ring on her finger throb and go warm.

Then – nothing.

She breathed again, then looked, a little fearfully, round the class.

Everyone, absolutely everyone, was staring at her in amazement.

* * * *

CHAPTER TWO

She didn't rub the ring to summon the genie back at once. So far he'd made her day a little *too* brilliant. Everyone had been staring at her in the wrong *sort* of amazement. She could do with a break.

The next hour passed with almost no interruption. No puffs of smoke. No angry showers of sparks. Only the ring on her finger getting warm over and over again, as if he were boiling with impatience inside it. So when Mr Piper said at the beginning of Art, "Call out your name if you need a paint jar," it was almost an accident that she was pulling at the hot little circle of gold just as she called out,

"Jeanie."

Puff! Flash! A column of drifting smoke, and he was there again, not bowing quite so deeply as before.

"Your wish?"

Jeanie flushed with annoyance. She felt a fool. It was one thing to conjure up a genie by accident, another to do it quite by mistake.

Unless, of course, you pretend that you did it on purpose. . .

Jeanie waved at her blank sheet of painting paper, and at the suggestion Mr Piper had written on the board: *The Most Beautiful Landscape*.

"Tell me," she said. "Which is the most beautiful landscape you have ever seen?"

The genie needed no prompting.

"Africa," he said. "Africa is *magnificent*. Africa is *dazzling*. Africa is *sublime*."

"You don't think it might have changed a bit since you last saw it?"

"Changed?" The genie stared. "Can burning plains and rolling grasslands change? Can razor-backed mountains fall flat? Shining waterfalls dry up as they tumble? Can mile on gleaming mile of sun-drenched beach fold up and disappear?"

Well. That seemed clear enough. Jeanie picked up her paintbrush.

"Go on, then," she said. "Fire ahead."

The genie shut his eyes. "Begin," he said, "by painting a lush river valley where comely antelope may dip their slender necks to sip from refreshing waters."

Jeanie was no born painter. Her lush river valley looked like something rather nasty spilled across a garage floor, her antelope like strange, long-eared maggots on peg legs.

Politely, the genie averted his eyes.

"Flamingoes!" he crooned gently, almost to himself, as his rich memories of Africa revived after centuries of sleep. "Tarantulas. Cobras. Pythons. Elephants!"

"I can't do animals," Jeanie complained.

The genie's lip curled.

"A large brown coconut?" he suggested rudely. "Perhaps a yam? Are they beyond my mistress's frail powers?"

Once again, Jeanie felt like swatting him off the desk.

"It's only *animals* I can't paint."

The light of challenge flashed in his eyes.

"Then paint me a tribal chief. Make him a magnificent African prince who wears his ceremonial robes, and armlets of carved wood, leafed with gold. Paint his bride at his side. Sprinkle her with gold dust!"

Jeanie laid down her paintbrush. Sprinkle her with gold dust! For heaven's sake! What did he think they *put* in school paintboxes? She was as cross with him as he was with her.

"*You* do it," she ordered him. "It is my wish. Paint me the dazzling African landscape, and the prince." Her eyes flashed, just like his. "And, at his side, paint me a lion so real it roars."

"So real it roars?"

"So real it roars!"

"Your whim – "

He didn't even finish. Or, if he did, the words were drowned by the fizz of a starry streak, bright as a comet's tail, which swept through the air and landed on her painting, changing it instantly.

"Grrrrrr*rr*!"

"Jeanie? Is that you?"

It was a fearsome lion and a fearsome roar, but Mr Piper was looking only at Jeanie.

"Gggrrrrrr*rrrrr*!"

"Jeanie! Please stop that silly noise at once!"

"GGGRRRRRRRRRRRRRRR!"

"*Jeanie!*"

Frantically, Jeanie twisted the ring. "Genie!" she whispered fiercely. "Disappear!"

A shower of sparks, and he was gone. On the desk, only a silly picture of a coconut, and, when she looked up, the whole class staring at her in amazement.

And, once again, it was the wrong sort.

* * * *

CHAPTER THREE

She was pleased and relieved when, half an hour later, Mr Piper strolled up and put the daily scribbled note from the school kitchen down on her desk.

"Jeanie," he said. "Your turn to copy out the lunch menu and help Mrs Handy set the tables."

Good! He couldn't be cross with her still, and it was a job she really enjoyed. She took the clean sheet of paper he offered her, and, reaching for her felt pens, wrote the date brightly across the top. Then, underneath, she copied out in fat and well-shaped letters (much neater than Mrs Handy's):

Shepherds' Pie
Salad
Fruit & Custard

There. Done. But Mrs Handy would not be coming to fetch it for a while. And so, to pass the time, she started decorating her menu around the edges with a delicate curlicue pattern she'd noticed on the genie's silk bodice. And soon her sheet of paper, too, began to look foreign and exotic and – well, yes – Arabian, as though you might raise your eyes from your prayer mat inside some shadowy mosque, and see the very same pattern repeated in cool tiles around the wall.

Thoughtfully she twisted the ring around her finger. It was as if the genie was, in some quite extraordinary way, much closer than she thought. Even in his absence he seemed to be giving her a hand with the border. She was still sitting quietly, twisting the ring round her finger and wondering, when Mrs Handy popped her head around the door.

"Who's helping today?"

"Me! Jeanie!"

Stupid of her not to lift her fingers off the ring as she called out her name! There was a sudden puff of glittering smoke, and the genie floated down onto the menu.

Startled, she snatched her hands back. The sheet of paper tore in half.

"Oh, no!" Jeanie wailed under her breath. "Now look what's happened!"

"A thousand pardons!" The genie was distraught. "Pelt me with desert roses! Starve me! Behead me!"

For heaven's sake! Starve him! Behead him! Jeanie did not even have time to scowl at him properly before Mrs Handy was calling from the doorway:

"Come along. Don't forget to bring the menu."

Obediently, Jeanie hurried towards the door. The genie leaped from desk to desk alongside her in vaporous somersaults, showering sparks over everyone sitting hunched over their workbooks. Nobody even noticed. Just for a moment, Jeanie felt a pang of envy. None of them had to worry about a genie! Why did she?

Ridiculous! Who could regret real magic when it came their way? She'd have a brilliant day. They'd all be staring at her in amazement – the right sort this time! And, as for the silly torn menu, what was a genie for if not to grant her every wish?

"Please," she said to him outside in the corridor. "I wish you'd make me a brand new menu."

"Allah is merciful!" cried the genie. "Lunchtime at last!"

He might have waited five hundred years for a meal, but Jeanie was in a hurry too.

"Quickly! A menu!"

The genie folded his arms, and bowed.

"Your slightest whim. . ."

Puff! *Flash*! The old torn sheet of paper disappeared, and a new menu was in her hand, complete with the very same patterned border. She was about to look at it, just to check, when Mrs Handy turned in the doorway to the lunchroom and reached out to take it.

Mrs Handy stared at Jeanie in amazement – the wrong sort.

"What's *this*?"

"Your menu."

Mrs Handy frowned. "Is it a joke?"

"A joke?" Jeanie was mystified.

Mrs Handy held out the menu, and Jeanie read:

Goat kebabs in a nest of crushed chick peas
Salad of petals of the desert rose
Pomegranates gathered at first blush of dawn

The genie glanced at it too.

"Lash me a thousand times!" he cried. "I have forgotten the olives bathed in essence of frankincense, without which no banquet could claim to be complete!"

Mrs Handy waved the menu in Jeanie's face.

"This isn't supposed to be a *banquet*," she said crossly. "It's a school dinner, and it's shepherds' pie!"

Fortunately for Jeanie, a violent hiss and rattling from the kitchen distracted her, and she rushed off.

The genie looked baffled.

"What does the fading blossom in the flowery apron *mean*?" he demanded. "All shepherds *love* goat kebabs."

"Not here they don't," Jeanie scolded him. "No one in this country eats goat."

"Really?" The genie was astonished. "No one at all?"

"No one at all."

"Strange!" said the genie, and fell into thoughtful silence. He looked, thought Jeanie, just a little bit homesick. But she'd no time to worry about that now.

"Come on. We have to set tables."

She hurried into the lunchroom. The tables were still pushed against the wall, the dishes still in piles on the china trolley, and it was five to twelve!

Well, what was the point of having a genie if he didn't help?

"Quick," she said. "Push all those tables together and lay out china."

The genie's eyes widened.

"Do my foolish ears deceive me?"

"Don't argue," Jeanie said. "Just lay out china."

The genie bowed.

"Your whim is my command."

The flash that filled the room was so brilliant it blinded Jeanie for a moment. She heard the windows rattle and felt the floor rock. Even to someone as unused to magic as she was, it seemed an awful lot of fuss to get a few plates laid on a few tables.

Warily she opened her eyes – and stared in horror.

The genie had pushed the tables together, and laid out China!

There was no doubt about it. It was China.

31

From the paper lanterns to the pagodas, from
the bamboo to the beansprouts, from the
moustaches to the mandarins, it was China.
Here, at one end, coolies were working in the
flooded paddy fields. There, at the other,
there was a tiny city. The curving rooftiles of
the houses shadowed the miniature court-

yards with their willow trees and clematis and camellias, their lotus pools and fish-ponds full of golden carp. And inside the tiny little houses, sitting amongst the silk hangings and the painted screens, were elegant women with long pins through their hair, and children in brightly-coloured quilted jackets.

From somewhere in the busy little city, a gong rang out loudly.

Mrs Handy's voice came through the dinner hatch.

"Stop ringing that dinner bell. I'm not quite ready yet."

Panicking, Jeanie swung round on the genie.

"Get rid of it!"

The genie seemed as hurt as he was astonished.

"Get rid of it? You haven't even *looked* at it properly yet. You haven't peeped through the windows to look at the the pottery figurines, or the porcelain vases, or the jade carvings. You haven't tasted any of the food."

Somersaulting onto a rooftop, showering sparks, he waved a hand.

"These people are eating too, you know. Bear's paw and baked owl and panther's breast. Not to mention all the boring old plain dishes like lotus roots and bamboo shoots and water chestnuts."

"Clear it away!"

Was he being deliberately awkward? He

took no notice of her pleas as he leaped effortlessly in a sprinkle of stars from one sloping rooftop to another.

"Got any aches and pains?" he taunted her. "The finest acupuncturist in Peking lives here. He'll take his long slim silver needles and – "

"Get rid of it!"

"You haven't even peeked in the opium den yet. . ."

Jeanie was furious.

"Make China disappear! I wear the ring! It is *my wish*!"

A scowl. Another blinding flash. The windows rattled in their frames. The floor rocked. China disappeared.

The hatch flew open.

"What *is* going on?"

"Sorry!" called Jeanie. She looked round for the china trolley. There was nothing on it.

She turned on the genie in a rage.

"Bring back that china!"

China immediately reappeared, with sampans floating down the Yangtze river.

"No, not that China! The *other* china!"

Jeanie was desperate. From the kitchen she could hear the sound of saucepans being scraped.

The genie smiled – not very pleasantly. And only as the hatch swung open and the clock hand reached twelve did he deign to wave a haughty hand.

Instantly, china plates lay in rows of military precision down both sides of the five tables.

"Ring the bell," called out Mrs Handy.

This was the job that everyone loved best. Jeanie ran for the bell. But even before she managed to lay a finger on it, the deep reverberations of an ancient Chinese gong rang through the room.

Jeanie spun round on him.

"You're spoiling everything!" she hissed.

"You and your magic! I think you're a whole lot more trouble than you're worth!"

The genie simply smiled, folded his arms, and bowed.

* * * *

CHAPTER FOUR

What could you do with a genie who hadn't had a meal for five hundred years? You couldn't order him back in a ring, could you? She had to take a chance and let him stay.

And it wasn't as bad as she expected. The first few moments were the worst. As Mrs Handy put the serving dish down on the table top, he came as close as he dared to its hot side, and stood on tip-toe peeping over the rim at the huge mound of shepherds' pie.

Tears sprang to his eyes like two bright little jewels, and he clutched his belly in all the torment of the oriental gourmet who has missed banquet after banquet for centuries, and then been offered lumpy mashed potato.

But he behaved. She didn't have to put up with him leaping in showers of silvery sparks around her plate. And the food was invisible from the moment he scooped it up in his fingers. She didn't see any of the other people at her table staring in astonishment as lumps of shepherds' pie rose in the air and vanished.

"My last school dinner!" said Asha, pushing her plate away. "Tomorrow I shall be in India."

The genie dropped the lump of potato he was holding, and sank to his knees beside Jeanie's plate.

"In–di–a!" It was a sigh of longing. "Oh, Allah! Be merciful! Transport me on the wings of my desire! Oh, India! How many times have I visited you – sweet land of pungent spices. Saffron! Coriander! Tamarind! Turmeric! Cardamom!"

Now the tiny little fellow was trying to push Jeanie's plate further away from him with his foot.

"Believe me, for one brass bowl of fragrant biriani, for one delicious chapati, I'd trade a bullock's cart of this pale mush my mistress offers me!"

"The food's so *different* in India," Asha said. "I've enjoyed my time here, but I shall be glad to be home again."

"Home!" mourned the genie. "Oh, Allah! Arabia, Africa, India – fly me anywhere you choose! The lush green valleys or the burning plains. The crowded cities or the cold high mountains. Anywhere but here!"

He sounded so sincere and desperate that Jeanie could scarcely bear it.

"I don't think any place is really better than another," she said aloud, hoping to console him.

"Home's home," said Asha.

"And blessings are surely heaped upon all those places without grey skies and mashed potato," added the genie.

Jeanie turned her face away. Outside, the rain beat steadily against the window panes. It must, she thought, be terrible to grow up, like Asha and the genie, in sun and heat and

baking dust, only to find yourself stuck in some chill damp place you'd never known.

As terrible as being raised with cool rain on your face and green underfoot, to find yourself in some scorched land where water was more precious than gold, and fierce sunlight hurt your eyes.

She'd hate that. She'd absolutely *hate* it. She'd be so homesick she would *die*.

Jeanie tore off the ring.

"Here!" she said to Asha. "Take it."

"*Take* it?"

"Yes. It's a present. It's for you. Take it. Put it on."

Everyone was staring at her in amazement.

"Please," she begged. "I want you to have it. I want to be able to think of you wearing it in India."

Asha spread her hands shyly.

"I couldn't. It's too – "

The genie was on his knees, pleading silently.

Jeanie gave the ring one last, tiny, secret rub.

"I *wish* you'd take it."

No one else saw the sudden puff of glittering smoke, or heard the genie's sigh of
ecstasy. But they all saw Asha reach out as
though bewitched, and, taking the ring, slip it
on her slim brown finger.

The genie turned to Jeanie. Folding his

arms, he gave his deepest bow in deepest gratitude. The look on his face was wonderful to see. Jeanie could tell that he was already lost in imagination, knowing his years of lonely imprisonment were over forever, and he would find himself spinning to glittering life time and again in cool courtyards and under shady banyan trees.

"Who gave you that?" people would forever be asking Asha.

"This ring?" She'd rub it without thinking. "Oh, *Jeanie.*"

And there he'd be, folding his arms and bowing, ready to serve. Until the day the ring slipped off her finger, and he moved on. What had he said? *There will always be someone. . .*

She could have kept him longer. But it would be like keeping a skylark in a tiny cage. Genies were creatures of colour and adventure. She'd read the Arabian Nights. You couldn't expect a genie who had known Sinbad the Sailor and Ali Baba and the forty thieves and Aladdin to be content with rainy skies and mashed potato.

No. Let him go, and wish him well on his travels back to India. . . Africa. . . Arabia. . . So many glorious hot places.

* * * *

CHAPTER FIVE

"In honour of Asha's last day," declared Mr Piper, "we shall all write about India."

Was it the pictures he lifted up to show them wind-whipped desert sands, and the moon hanging like a curved blade over ancient walls?

Or was it the genie secretly blowing one of his magical glittering circles around her head?

For it seemed like a memory, what Jeanie found herself writing about – afternoons so hot and still it seemed that you might run a sword through the air and part it like a thick curtain. It seemed like a memory, what she wrote about the monsoon – the hot winds blowing day and night from the huge open plains, then clouds that banked up till you could hardly bear the sense of waiting any longer. And then suddenly the rains came down with all the force of stones, until the ground sprang lush and green all around, and life burst out, with frogs and toads hopping in hundreds. Snakes! Cockroaches! And a million insects!

She'd never written so much in her life.

After she'd finished, Mr Piper picked it up, and read it aloud to everyone.

"Marvellous!" he kept saying. "Wonderful!"

Asha was staring into space, as if she were already home. The bell rang for the end of school, but everyone sat enchanted in their seats, as Mr Piper read on about the chime of temple bells and the sweet smell of incense and strings of flowers. And women in silk saris with silver bangles tinkling on their wrists and ankles, and ancient dances so precise there are a hundred separate movements for hands and eyes. And carpet weavers, snake charmers, basket makers. And holy men and horoscopes. And sweets and festivals. Everything – everything you might miss if you were far away for five hundred years.

And, as they listened, everyone stared at Jeanie in amazement – the right sort this time.

"Brilliant!" breathed Asha. "That is *exactly* how it is!"

Mr Piper patted Jeanie on the back.

"Well done. Well done!"

As Asha packed up her few things, the ring on her finger seemed to be glowing. Jeanie couldn't help glancing at it a little wistfully. But why be sorry she was letting him go? He'd made things awkward for her all day long. He'd never fit in – not in his growing fever of homesickness. He'd be a lot more trouble than magic was worth.

And he had granted her wish. He'd given her a brilliant day. He'd done his very best. Goodbye and good luck to him.

Just then, Asha came up to say goodbye.

Jeanie smiled as she squeezed the hand that wore the precious ring.

"Good luck. Goodbye." she said. "Goodbye. Good luck."

You'd think, to hear her, she was parting from two people, not just one.

And the ring glowed on Asha's finger as she walked out.

* * * *

A Sudden Swirl
of Icy Wind

CHAPTER ONE

William was in the worst trouble. He was shaking as Granny towered over him, her arms folded and her face dark with rage.

"William!"

He was upset, and close to tears. But he wasn't sorry, not a bit. He had done nothing wrong. In fact, he'd been specially good, keeping himself busy in Granny's smart front room, where all the chairs were fat and stuffed and shiny, and everywhere you looked there were spindly little tables with tops as brown and gleaming as conkers, and fancy ornaments wobbling on top of them.

1

He hadn't knocked anything over. Nothing was broken. Nothing was even cracked. And she knew he was in here, playing with the gun he'd been given for Christmas yesterday. Mum knew he was in here, too. She had crept up on him before she left for work. She'd done one of her special vampire goodbyes, swooping to wrap him in her huge dark and flapping nurse's cloak, sinking her fangs in his soft throat.

He'd wriggled free as usual, and given her a proper kiss.

"See you tonight," she'd told him. "It's a pity that hospitals can't stop for Christmas."

Then she was off, doing her Dracula imitation on the way to the car, startling all Granny's neighbours. He'd waved from the window, then, when the car was out of sight, he'd started to prise the lid off the box that held his new gun. Granny poked her head round the door and saw him. She wasn't angry then. All she'd said was, "Happy, William?"

He'd nodded. Yes, he was happy. He'd got what he wanted most for Christmas, and he had all morning free. He knew there was more than half the cake left, and he'd be given an enormous slice as soon as Granny decided it was time for coffee. And there were game shows he liked on television later. Granny's television was much better than the one at home. So he was lucky to be here.

That's what he thought. The silver hands on the clock slid round silently as William played. Half past nine. Ten o'clock. Quarter past ten. William was getting hungrier. And then, at last, he heard Granny's footsteps tap along the hall and down the steps that led to the front room. And she was standing in the open doorway.

He turned to smile at her, and show her what he'd been doing all morning, out from under her feet, being no trouble. Proudly he said:

"Look! See what I can do. See how –"

But then he heard Granny's little gasp of shock, and saw the look on her face. First she went red, then her face darkened with rage.

"William!"

He stared.

"Just *what* do you think you are doing?"

Baffled, he looked down at the gun in his hand. But she didn't wait for an answer.

"How dare you, William!"

He couldn't think what was wrong. She knew he had the gun. She'd watched him unwrapping it beside the Christmas tree. She'd even admired the flashes of silver lightning on the handle.

"But –"

"I can't believe my eyes! So naughty! Dreadful! Shocking!"

"But, Granny –"

4

"No, William! I don't want to hear any silly excuses. I just want you to say that you're sorry."

"But –"

"Say you're sorry, William."

She stood with folded arms, waiting. William was mystified. He couldn't for the life of him work out what he'd done wrong. He hadn't made a mess or a noise. He'd been no trouble at all, just practising firing his gun over and over again, getting better and better. What was so wrong about *that*?

"William! I'm waiting!"

He glowered down at his shoes. What was she so mad about? Nothing was broken. Why *should* he say he was sorry? What had he *done*?

"William! I am still waiting!"

But William was still glowering at his shoes. No reason why he should be bullied into saying something that he didn't mean. It would be just a lie. He wasn't sorry. He was just a bit rattled with Granny standing there saying "How *dare* you?" over and over again. But how dare she try to bully someone into telling a lie?

5

"I'm not sorry," he muttered sullenly.

"What was that, William?"

"I said I'm not sorry!"

He didn't mean to shout it out like that. It came out loud because he was hurt and angry and a little bit frightened. He'd never seen Granny like this before. Even when he was younger and smashed her lovely china bowl of roses, doing cartwheels down the hall, she'd only blamed herself for leaving it on the table. She hadn't been angry with him. Nothing like this.

He scowled at her. She wasn't being fair.

To his dismay, she reached out and caught his arm, pulling him towards the door.

"In that case, young man, you can just sit by yourself for a while, and think it over till you *are* sorry."

She steered him across the hall towards the little room filled with old junk thrown in there years and years ago, when William's grandfather died. Tugging the door open, she pushed William in. He didn't struggle. He didn't dare. He just let her propel him forward, into the clutter. The door banged behind him, and he tripped over grandfather's

6

old sea chest, scraping his knees. He picked himself up from the floor, shaking a little, and was just sitting down on the sea chest when he heard Granny's last words coming sharply through the panels of the door:

"And don't come out till you can say you're sorry!"

Well, it would be a long wait! William had heard it often enough when he refused to wear a coat, or eat green beans, or go round to play with someone he didn't like much: "You're as stubborn as your grandfather!" It was supposed to be a joke, but it would serve Granny right if he was, and she had to wait all day.

And, sitting on the sea chest, William began to wonder for the first time in his life about the grandfather he'd never known, the famous Captain Flook. He swivelled round to take a long look at the portrait hanging, a little crooked, on the storeroom wall. Captain Flook stared out of the knobbly old wooden frame, bearded and grave. The polished buttons on his uniform caught the light, along with bands of gold lace round his sleeves, and the gold oak leaves on the peak of his cap. He was a fine-looking man. But stubborn and secretive, Granny said. If he didn't want her to know about something, he would just say: "That's between me and Mustapha".

Whatever that meant.

And this was grandfather's trunk. William had never had the chance to be alone in this room before. Granny came in sometimes to

root through the clutter of broken telescopes and cracked ships' bells, musty books in strange languages and conch shells from far-away beaches. She might be searching for a tiny spyglass so she could see better at the pantomime; or she might be hunting for some bag of old coins or pebbles or foreign stamps, to keep William busy for an afternoon. But she would always leave him in the doorway.

"Don't come in any further, William. It's such a *mess.*"

So he'd never even looked in the trunk. What could be in it? It was a proper chest made of stout wood, with firm brass bands to hold it fast through all sea weathers. The clasps were stiff, and hard to lift. He'd bruise his fingers trying to prise them up. But he was determined to raise the lid and have a look inside. He'd use the edge of this strange sliver of flint, here on the floor. He'd twist it between the two halves of the clasp, and –

A sudden swirl of icy wind seemed to gust out of the chest. It smelled, quite unmistakably, of sea. William had stood often enough on slippery green rocks, staring out at the far horizon and the waves. He'd smelt the tang of sea wind and licked the salt taste of it from his lips. This was the very same wind, but it was leaking somehow out of grandfather's trunk, as William struggled to open it.

Impossible! Wind didn't *keep*. After so many years, the untouched trunk should have inside it nothing but still, stale air.

William redoubled his efforts. Gritting his teeth, he pushed harder and harder. He grunted with effort and hurt his fingers, but finally the catches gave. And with a cry of triumph

William pushed one last time, heaving until the rounded lid swung over backwards with its own great weight, and hit the floor with a crash.

The smell of sea filled the whole room. The air around was suddenly chilly and windy and wet and fresh, and William could taste salt spray.

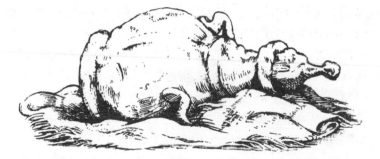

And there, inside the trunk, lying on rotting sacks, was an old bottle. An old green bottle, made of glass, but of a glass so ancient and dark and pitted that William could not begin to guess what might be hidden inside it.

11

Gingerly he rolled it over on the sacking. It felt chill to the touch. What was inside? As Granny said, his grandfather was far too secretive. He should have labelled it. Then William would not have had to lift it out – oh, so carefully – and hold it, colder than a stone in his hand, while he twisted at the encrusted glass stopper. What was it grandfather always said when he chose to keep a secret?

"That's between me and Mustapha."

Such a curious thing to say. So foreign and exotic. And suddenly William found himself softly saying the word aloud, testing the strangeness of it out on his own tongue.

"Mustapha."

Then, just a little louder:

"Mustapha."

Then, louder still:

"Mustapha. Mustapha! *Mustapha*!"

There was another swirl of icy wind. The smell of salt grew stronger, and William could have sworn he heard the lonely cry of a sea bird. The room seemed to heave, as if the floorboards had become a ship's deck, and the storeroom itself was suddenly afloat on the high seas.

Then, with a crack, the stopper of the bottle split in two. Each half of shattered glass began to melt into a mist, green as the bottle itself. And from the bottle poured more mist, and more and more, until it was as thick as fog, and a green pillar of it coiled and rose, up and up, higher and higher, until it was high as the ceiling.

As William stared, the thick green fog gathered itself into a shape, the strangest shape, a towering and turbaned man of mist. His chest was beefy and his shoulders broad.

13

His arms were folded across his massive body. But in the coiling vapour of his lower half, there were no legs at all, not even the shape of them. Only a spiral of thinning green mist, trailing back into the bottle.

The vision towered above William.

"I am Mustapha," he said. "The genie of the bottle. Someone has called me."

CHAPTER TWO

Transfixed with terror and astonishment, William could not speak. The genie loomed above him. After a moment's silence, he spoke again.

"You have only to command me."

But command him what? To pour the vapour of himself back in the bottle, safe out of sight, and bring the world to rights again? Well, not to rights, exactly. Nothing was right today. And, thinking this, William stood still and silent as, one by one, tears of fright and exhaustion rolled down his cheeks.

The genie unfolded his beefy arms and, leaning over, reached down to touch William's cheek with a chilly mist finger. He lifted a tear.

"You are in trouble."

It wasn't even a question. But still William nodded.

The genie glanced round the storeroom.

"Where are the sofas of feathers and rose petals?" he asked. "The silken hangings and the swaying fans? The sweet music and the lovely dancing girls? The jugs of wine, the dishes of fat geese drowned in sweet berry sauce? Are you *imprisoned*?"

If you looked at it that way, thought William, he practically was. And awash with misery and self-pity, he somehow couldn't help nodding a second time.

"Tell me your gaoler's name!" the genie cried. "Prayers and regrets shall be out of season! I shall heap piles of stones upon his head!"

"Actually, it's my granny," said William.

"Your own grandmother! You astonish me! Tell me to wing her to a stony place inhabited by wolves. Her body shall be carrion for the crows, prey for the beasts!"

"She didn't mean it," William said hastily. "Honestly. She was just a bit cross."

"Cross?"

16

"Well . . . Furious, really."

The genie settled himself more comfortably on his spiralling coils of mist, and listened carefully as William, gradually pushing aside his fear of the huge shape towering above him, explained how the trouble had started. How, by the time Granny poked her head round the door to invite him for cake and coffee, he had been practising with the gun for hours, firing the six little pellets over and over again, getting better and better, till, if he aimed at the tiny plastic cow, then that was the only animal that fell over. And if he aimed at the little man with the crook, the shepherd, it was he who went spinning over backwards onto the cotton wool snow. If he aimed at the angel, she tumbled off the stable roof. And if he closed one eye and kept his hand as steady as possible, he could even hit something as small as the legs of the ox and ass's feeding trough, and send the tiny plastic baby, in a shower of straw, catapulting out of the manger.

"Manger?" The genie's look of bafflement was turning slowly into one of shock. "Did you say 'Shepherd? Angel? Ox and ass? *Manger?*'"

"They're only plastic," said William. "And

they're not even new. And every time I'd knocked them down, I set them all up again, exactly the same. I even picked all of the straw off the carpets. I can't imagine why she made such a fuss."

He looked up to see the genie's face darkening with rage. All William's terror returned. What could a genie do if he lost his temper? Did he have to wait for a command? Perhaps, now he finally realised just how unfair William's granny had been, he might suddenly wing her away and heap her with stones.

"She's usually very nice," said William. "She's usually very patient."

"Powers of heaven!" the genie cried. He seemed to be swelling as if, as his anger grew, he had to grow to hold it. "Clearly if your grandmother's patience was as deep as the sea, you would still try to swim beneath it."

It took William a moment to make sense of this. But when he understood what Mustapha meant, he was indignant.

"Why pick on *me*? What have *I* done?"

The genie looked at him with deep disdain.

"It seems, to start, you have been born when wits were scant."

"Are you calling me stupid?"

The genie folded his arms and stared imperturbably into space.

"*Jawab ul ahmaq sakut*," he murmured. "The only answer to a fool is silence."

William was no coward. And he was suddenly sick of everyone around him folding their arms and going dark in the face for no good reason he could understand. So, folding his own arms in insolent imitation, and glaring up at the genie in his turn, he shouted at him:

"I have only to command you. That's what

19

you said. I command you to stop being rude, and answer me. What have I done wrong?"

The genie glanced down. Was he taken with William's courage, or his foolhardiness? Whichever it was, the look on his face suddenly changed, softening from haughty contempt to interest in this boy who had the boldness to stand up and bellow at a genie whose powers of enchantment had, over centuries, held kings and sultans in awe.

And then he pursed his lips, and blew. A sudden swirl of icy wind chilled the room, making poor William shiver. And, as he watched, the genie began to shrink. First William thought Mustapha had decided to disappear. Then he realised the genie was simply choosing to blow the bulk of his damp self away, and make himself smaller. Harder and harder the genie blew, and the wind swept round colder and colder. Mustapha sank – lower, lower, lower – till, man-sized, he settled comfortably on Captain Flook's trunk.

"Come. Sit beside me on your father's sea chest."

William hesitated before daring to correct him.

"It was my grandfather's. And he died a long time ago."

Mustapha sighed.

"Life is a splendid robe," he said. "Its only fault is its short length."

William perched nervously on the very edge of the chest, and tried to reply in Mustapha's own way of speaking.

"Your robe must be quite long, though."

The genie stared, unsmiling, back through centuries, and into ages yet to come.

"The robe of enchantment has neither seams nor hem."

Did he mean that a genie lives forever? That would explain how he could rise from a trunk in which he'd wasted years and years, and not seem to mind about half a lifetime missed.

William pointed to the portrait.

"So it was grandfather you knew?"

"And his father. And his father, too. Men of honoured memory." Mustapha pointed an accusing finger at William. "Not one of them would shame himself the way you have today."

William spread his hands in exasperation.

"What have I *done*?"

"A droplet of advice," the genie said. "A

man's religion is like his table. One eats off fine white linen, another off scrubbed wood. Some set a feast, and others eat only the most simple dishes. This man will eat in silence, and these ladies eat with song and dance. Would you spit in the food?"

"Spit in the food? Of course not!"

The genie fell silent and waited while William thought. Did what the genie said make any sense? Had he done something as horrid and upsetting as spitting in someone's food? William thought back. It was true that Granny cared about her battered nativity stable and the little figures. Each year she lifted them carefully from the box, and set them up on the side where everyone could see them. And after Christmas she packed them away just as carefully. They certainly weren't expensive. William had seen them often enough in the shops, and they were half the price of those fierce fighting figures everyone in his class used to collect and paint, before they took up with the guns. So they must be precious in a different way. And the longer William sat quietly beside Mustapha, thinking about it, the clearer it all was.

Granny went to church. She went at Easter
and at Christmas, and sometimes on Sundays.
She kept a cross beside the bed, and she'd
been married in church. And once, when the
film of Jesus's life came on television, she'd
asked William to sit quietly or slip off somewhere else. She was a Christian. She believed
in God, and she believed Jesus was God's son.
So that tiny plastic baby in the manger meant
something to Granny. Something very important. Mustapha was right. Flipping it head

24

over heels with a pellet from a gun was probably even ruder and more hurtful than spitting in food.

William felt terrible – shabby and thoughtless and ashamed. More tears forced their way out and rolled down his cheeks, and, once again, the genie stretched out a finger to catch one.

"Another droplet of advice," he said. "He that respects not cannot be respected."

"I feel simply awful," said William.

The genie smiled.

"May Allah dry your tears and raise your spirits. Wisdom walks slowly, but her steps are sure."

William was unconvinced.

"You said grandfather, and his father, and his father too, would never shame themselves the way I have today."

"No family rocks nothing but angels in the cradle," the genie said. "Perhaps Captain Flook the Adventurer lives a second time in you."

"Which one was he?"

The genie shrugged, and William realised Mustapha neither knew nor cared how many fathers' fathers came between William and Captain Flook the Adventurer. Again he seemed to stare back, through centuries of magic, to grander days in his own land.

"Tell me," said William, settling on an old rug rolled on the floor beside the sea chest. "Tell me the story."

The genie stirred.

"You have only to command me . . ."

CHAPTER THREE

"Your great, great, great, great, great –" He hesitated a moment, and then shrugged. "One of your grandfathers –"

"Of honoured memory!"

"Was a fine sailor called Captain Flook the Adventurer. And he commanded a fine ship and followed the four winds on seas blackened by storm and frosted by moonlight. He took his ship further than any other, past where the whales whistle and the porpoises roll, and he was always the first to see strange things."

William hugged his knees.

"I know," he said. "Granny has an embroidery hanging above her bed. I learned it when I had chicken pox. It says: *They that go down to the sea in ships, and do business in great waters, these see the works of the Lord and his wonders in the deep.*"

"Exactly so," agreed Mustapha. "And Captain Flook saw many wonders and sailed many seas. But no man holds the wind in his hands, and there came a day when not a breath stirred in his ship's sails. And another day. And another. And for weeks afterwards the ship rocked only at the mercy of the waves, while the tar bubbled in her seams from the heat, and the decks cracked, and the crew turned from men to living skeletons. Then, out of spite, a wind rose into a cruel squall which tore the sails into a thousand pieces, and drove the ship on rocks, and all the men that were not starved were drowned."

"But not him."

"Not him. A wave lifted her white neck, and dropped the Captain on the sands of an island. And it was there, searching for water, that Captain Flook found an old bottle –"

"And pulled out the stopper!"

"And freed your servant from a thousand years of idleness."

William closed his eyes as Mustapha told his story, and saw the mist that poured out of the bottle, causing Captain Flook to stumble back on the shingle in his astonishment. He saw the fog that rose, up, up and up, making the sea boil, till it reached high as the clouds and towered darkly over the ocean and the land, before it took its ancient, magic shape.

"Was he as scared as I was?"

"He did me the honour of appearing so."

"And when he stopped being frightened, what did he want?"

Mustapha snorted.

"Trifles and toys: jugs of crystal water, a loaf of bread; and afterwards rubies, sapphires, riches of all kinds – oh, and of course, a magic carpet."

"To fly to a safe place!"

"No place boasts safety." The genie shook his head. "I bring a man only the lesser gifts of treasure and luxury. The two great gifts are not within my power."

"The two great gifts. What are they?"

"Wisdom and Life."

William thought about it for a moment. It made sense. Then he looked up, and saw Mustapha watching him with a little smile.

"Go on," William ordered. "Carry on with the story."

The genie bowed his head.

"You have only to command me. The carpet flew over India and over Persia. It flew over Syria and Egypt, and all of Arabia. It flew over a dozen great deserts and a dozen great cities. And all the while Captain Flook the Adventurer was hungry for more treasures: bags of gold, strings of pearls, dishes of diamonds. And he piled them round him on the magic carpet till he was satisfied at last. And then he leaned over and pointed to a courtyard far below, with fountains and shady palm trees."

"And that's where you brought the carpet down to land."

"Indeed, he had only to command me. The carpet circled the high minaret tower on which the muezzin stood, calling the faithful to prayer. And it came gently to rest on firm ground, under the branches of a spreading tamarind tree."

"Were the people astonished to see him?"

"Nobody saw."

"Was no one there?"

"The courtyard was filled with people. It was noon on the last day of the week, and everyone had come to pray. There were so many worshippers that those who could not fit inside the mosque had unfolded their prayer mats on the stones of the courtyard."

"To make their own little holy place!"

"To make their own little holy place. And, turning towards Mecca, their holiest place of all, they said their prayers to Allah the Beneficent, the Merciful, bowing their heads to the ground."

"And so they didn't notice Captain Flook."

"No. They were deep in prayer. And he, dizzy from flying through air, didn't see them. He stood and stretched and yawned, and felt the good hard ground beneath his feet. And his thoughts turned at once to his treasures, and what they might be worth. So hastily gathering up all the gems he could, Captain Flook stepped out of the shade into sunlight."

"Didn't they notice him then?"

"No. But now, at last, the Captain noticed them. For at that very moment the Minister of the Mosque, the Imam, began to read aloud from the holy book. *'The east and the west is God's,'* he declared. *'Therefore, whichever way you turn, there is the face of God. Truly, God is immense and knowing.'"*

"It sounds like something Granny might embroider," said William.

Mustapha shrugged. "A Christian reads the Bible, a Moslem the Koran, a Jew the Torah. Lose one book, and you could reach God with another. The stones that build all the great faiths are much the same. Only the rooftiles and the decorations differ. I have seen good men everywhere, and everywhere a good man is known for what he is."

"So they wouldn't mind the Captain being in their courtyard?"

"Not in the slightest. The Captain would have been welcome. But when he heard the Imam's voice, he spun around in surprise. The dish of gems flashed in the fierce sunlight, and the Captain was dazzled. Stumbling, he showered over the bent backs of the worshippers a cascade of diamonds and emeralds, sapphires and amethysts, rubies and opals, crystals and pearls."

William's eyes widened.

"Did he go after them?"

"Indeed he did." Mustapha's lip curled. "Scrabbling and snatching, tripping and cursing."

"Cursing?"

"Yes, cursing. Even as the faithful were at prayer."

It made shooting little pellets at a plastic crib look like pretty mild stuff. William felt rather cheered as Mustapha went on with the story of how Captain Flook the Adventurer fell in such deep trouble.

"At first, no one moved, such was their shock and disgust. Then, as even the Captain realised his foolishness, and left off his hunt for gems, there was the most terrible silence. The only sound to be heard was the faint clatter of a diamond here, the soft roll of a pearl there. And then, as the Imam took up his reading of the Koran again, Little Cassim Ali who sold burnt peas in the market place leaped to his feet. He signalled to his friend Zantout, who watered the streets to lay the dust. And together they turned their eyes on Abou Mekares who was the strongest man in the Caliph's guard. And without a word the three of them seized Captain Flook, who had only a moment to kick the old green bottle safely away under the tamarind tree."

"Where did they take him?"

35

"To the prison nearby, where he was locked up so that he could no longer disturb their holy prayers."

"Just like me, really," said William. "And for upsetting people in exactly the same way."

"As I dared to suggest," Mustapha reminded him. "Perhaps the Captain lives a second time in you."

"We've got it a bit better this time, then," said William. "Being stuck in here can't be half as bad as being in prison."

Mustapha raised an eyebrow.

"Forgive me," he murmured. "But truth is not hid in a nutmeg. Compared with this place, the prison was a palace brimming with pleasure and luxury."

Maybe the storeroom wasn't the best room in Granny's house. Or the tidiest. But even so, William felt duty bound to defend it.

"That isn't very polite. How could a prison be better than here?"

In answer, Mustapha just murmured:

"*Kas na guyad ki dugh-i-man tursh ast . . .*"

"What does that mean?"

"Nobody calls his own buttermilk sour . . ."

William was irritated.

"Tell me," he ordered, "how Captain Flook could be better off in his prison than I am here."

Mustapha bowed his head. "You have only to command me. First, in his prison Captain Flook found a dish of weevils feasting on rotten barley bread. Here, there is nothing – indeed, a man's belly might begin to fear his throat was cut."

37

William was still unravelling this when Mustapha continued:

"Second, in prison the Captain had the company of forty learned men. Here, before I arose –"

"Forty learned men? In a *prison*?"

"Most certainly. And most learned. All doctors."

"All doctors! How?"

"Perfectly simple. The Caliph was weak and sickly. So with the rising of each moon, he summoned a doctor and demanded a cure. Then, as the moon waned and he felt no better, he threw the doctor in prison."

"Forty doctors, though! That's longer than three years of being ill. What on earth was wrong with him?"

Mustapha sniffed.

"Everything and nothing. Nothing and everything. Everything because the man was weak almost to death. Nothing because the cause was a lifetime of idleness. The Caliph had young girls to fan him and young boys to lift the spoon up to his lips. He had women to bring him his robes and dress him, and men to carry him from place to place. From the moment his honoured mother gave him birth, the feet of the Caliph had never touched the ground."

"Never touched the ground!" William was shocked. "I don't believe it!"

"I can assure you that it was the truth. The soles of his slippers were made of the finest silver tissue."

William rocked on the carpet, hugging his knees and gazing at his own tough winter shoes. Slippers of silver tissue! Ridiculous! Glancing up at Mustapha, he asked:

"Didn't any of the doctors *notice*? Didn't they *guess*?"

"Guess? They were all fine doctors. They all *knew*. But none of them dared say."

It made sense. William would not have wanted to be the first to tell a mighty Caliph that he was actually a lazy slug.

"Tricky . . ."

A hint of admiration crept into Mustapha's voice.

"It was a puzzle to test even a genie's powers. And I, alas, was trapped in my bottle under the tamarind tree. But Captain Flook was a resourceful man, and he who must face the terrors of tides and rocks and angry seas must learn courage and quick wits. So when the Captain heard the doctors' story, he stood and rattled the bars of the prison, and shouted for the guard.

'Take me to the Caliph!' he roared.

'Why?' laughed the guard. 'Is your body in such a hurry to say farewell to your head?'

'Take me to the Caliph!' roared the Captain again. 'Or it will be your head rolling over stones, not mine. I have sailed across a dozen seas to bring the Caliph a cure for his weakness.'

'A cure for the Caliph's weakness?' The whisper ran around the prison walls. 'He brings a cure across a dozen seas.'"

William looked up.

"I bet the guard took him to the Caliph pretty sharpish once he heard that."

Mustapha agreed.

"So fast the Captain barely saw the chambers of polished black marble through which he was hurried. And, finally, he stood before the Caliph."

"What did the Caliph say?"

"Hardly a word. The Caliph lay on a sofa of the finest brocade. Too weak to raise head or finger, he simply whispered:

'Give me the cure.'

'Alas,' said the Captain. 'I cannot give it to you. For the cure is the key of good health, and it lies buried in your palace garden.'

'Send for it quickly,' whispered the Caliph. 'For I am weak almost to death.'

'Alas,' said the Captain. 'The key to good health cannot be found by another. The one who digs for it, and finds it, takes the cure.'

"The Caliph lay back, exhausted and disappointed, as his last hopes drained from his

41

face. But the Captain had quite as much to lose as the Caliph in this matter, so he stepped forward.

'Come,' he said in the voice that had soothed many a ship's boy through his first tempest. 'Let us go in the garden and look for the key.'"

"And did he go?"

"Trembling, the Caliph took the weight of his body on his own feet for the first time in his life. As he stepped forward, resting on the Captain's arm, the slippers of silver tissue fell away in shreds. Barefoot, he shuffled weakly down the marble steps, into the garden. And there the Captain took a spade from the hand of an astonished gardener, and handed it to the Caliph.

'Dig.'

'Where?' asked the Caliph, spilling hot tears in his weakness. 'The garden is huge. Where shall I find this key of good health?'

'Alas, nobody knows.'

'But,' cried the horrified Caliph. 'I might dig the whole garden before I find it!' He turned to the Captain, but the Captain simply bowed his head, and stood in silence. And so, slowly and sadly, the Caliph lifted the heavy spade and let

it drop in the earth. Slowly and sadly he bore his weight down on the handle, lifting a clod of dry earth. Slowly and sadly he bent over and sifted through it.

'Nothing,' he said.

'Try again,' begged the Captain in the voice that had encouraged many a ship's boy up the highest mast. And, strengthened, the Caliph dug – once, twice, three times – until the Captain said:

'Enough. Let us rest. The key of good health will not disappear. We'll dig again tomorrow.'"

William was grinning hugely.

"Brilliant!" he interrupted Mustapha. "Brilliant! And did the Caliph go out and dig the garden every day?"

Mustapha chuckled in turn. "Every day for a whole month. And every morning he asked the Captain: 'Shall we find the key of good health today?' And every morning the Captain replied: 'Perhaps, if we dig deep enough and long enough.'"

"And the Caliph got stronger and stronger!"

"The weakness dripped from him as from a melting rose sherbert. His flabby arms grew muscled and strong. His soft belly vanished. His legs grew wiry and brown. Some days he dug for hours and, in the sheer pleasure of digging, forgot the key."

"And the Captain didn't remind him?"

"Not for a moment. The Captain lolled on the steps of the fountain, sipping lush wines and trying to decide if Fatima, the jewel of the harem, would make a sailor's wife. Sometimes, watching the Caliph dig, he felt his own muscles weakening from disuse, and, leaping up, he'd try to wrestle the spade from the Caliph's hand."

44

"Wrestle it?"

"Indeed, yes. The Caliph had become a strong man with all his digging. Not wishing to give up the spade, he'd wrestle back. And the two men might struggle happily for hours over one spade, till one day the grand vizier tired of the sight and, without thinking, sent for another. As soon as the Caliph saw it, he cried: 'What? Another spade? But then the Captain might be the lucky man who finds the key of good health!'

'Sovereign of the Faithful,' said the grand vizier, shaking his head. 'Do you not know that you do not *need* the key any longer?' The Caliph stared at the grand vizier in amazement. Then he looked down at his strong lean arms and his firm legs, and tears of happiness sprang in his eyes, and he turned to Captain Flook the Adventurer.

'Ask me for anything,' he said. And, promptly, the Captain answered:

'Give me a ship, a wife, and that old green bottle that lies under the tamarind tree in the courtyard beside the great mosque.'"

"And so the Caliph let him go?"

"He was a man of honour. He kept his word."

"And the three of you sailed off."

"We all sailed off. The Captain sailed proudly, bathed in the heartfelt praises and grateful blessings of all the Caliph's people. Fatima sailed with her eyes tightly closed, pale as a grub, leaning over the ship's rail. And I lay, greener than mist, inside the sea chest on a bed of the finest brocade."

"That rotten sacking?"

"It is past its best."

"Why didn't the Captain let you out of the bottle? You could have helped poor Fatima."

Mustapha smiled.

"The Captain had learned his lesson. A gift given brings very little and does not last. A gift earned brings more, and lasts a lifetime.

Fatima opened her eyes after a week, and saw the dolphins wheeling and leaping in the high green seas."

"His wonders in the deep . . ."

Mustapha bowed his head.

"Lakum dinukum wa li dini," he murmured. "To you your religion, and to me mine."

"What if you haven't got one?" William was thinking about himself and his mother.

Mustapha shrugged.

"What a man thinks, or does not think, is his own business. It's what a man does in the world that counts."

Mum was all right, then. She spent half her life up at the hospital, stitching up cuts and helping frightened people. He wasn't quite so sure about himself, going round upsetting people. The memory of Granny's folded arms and dark face came back to William in a horrid rush.

"I'm not doing so well, am I? Granny was so angry. Grabbing my arm and pulling me along and pushing me in here " He sighed. "But now that I know what upset her, I think I could say sorry."

Mustapha sniffed.

"And she could usefully return the favour."

"What? Granny? Say sorry to *me*?"

William was amazed.

"Why not?" Mustapha shook a finger towards the door. "Grey hairs do not come woven into a halo. And no one should go poking in another's bag, looking for sins. These things are best left to God."

Mustapha had a point. There were enough religions in the world, and they all cared about different things – here a cross, there a scroll; what you ate, how you dressed, which way you faced when you were praying, words you said. You couldn't keep everyone's rules if you tried. You would always be in trouble with *someone*.

"And Granny didn't even bother to try to explain, before she lost her temper."

Suddenly Mustapha seemed bored with the whole sorry business. He yawned a small cavern of mist. And another.

"For every believer found sitting peaceably in God's house, you will find three more fighting on the steps," he said. "As you will see when you are old enough to go to sea."

"Me? Go to sea?"

Mustapha stared. A sudden swirl of icy wind chilled the room. Was he annoyed? Certainly the look on his face had turned to stone.

"Are you a Flook? Or are you not?"

"Well, yes. I suppose I am. I'm William Flook –"

William broke off. Mustapha was swelling – up and out and off the sea chest towards the ceiling. The cry of gulls rang in William's ears. The floorboards heaved. There was a salt taste on his lips and, far away, he could hear the crash of surf.

Filling the room with his sea mist, Mustapha roared:

"Am I to lie *forever* in this trunk? How many Flooks must live and die before I see again the crescent moons and desert sands of my first days?"

"I'll take you back!" cried William. He'd promise anything. Anything to stop the sound of surf crashing on rocks, harder and harder, so any moment Granny would appear at the door. "I'll take you back, I swear. If I'm a sailor, you'll see them with me. If not, I'll go once and leave the bottle there."

"Your word on it!"

The genie stretched down to William a clammy hand of mist. His piercing eyes were green as deepest seas, and, as if hypnotized by the sheer power of his glance, William tucked his own hands safely behind his back, and lowered his head.

"You have only to command me," he said simply.

Mustapha laughed. The laughter echoed as he gathered himself up on his coils of mist. It turned to the harsh cry of a sea bird as, with another swirl of icy wind, he spun around, pouring himself back in the bottle. Faster and faster he spun. And as the mist flowed downwards, clearing the air and emptying the room, the cry of the sea bird grew fainter and fainter, more and more far away. Until, as the last wisps of green mist formed themselves into a stopper, and hardened instantly to pitted glass, the room was filled with silence.

"William?"

William turned. Granny was standing in the doorway, looking anxious.

"William, what was that noise? Are you all right?"

He looked down at the bottle, lying so harmlessly on its bed of rotten sacking. *Was* it the finest brocade, past its best? Was –? Did –? Had –?

There would be time enough. And there'd be time to keep his promise, too. Carefully, William lifted the heavy lid of the sea chest and swung it over, shutting the bottle away.

He turned to face Granny.

"I'm sorry if what I was doing upset you. I didn't realise."

"I'm sorry I was so angry. I didn't think."

She stretched out her arms. Gratefully, William walked towards her. She slid an arm round his shoulders as they strolled out of the room together. There was still time for cake and coffee and the game shows on television. His mother would be back later. The day was saved. As for the future, William had time to think about that. There was no need to talk about it now. After all, William found himself thinking as they walked down the hall, 'That's between me and Mustapha'.

Whatever that meant.

A Sudden Glow of Gold

CHAPTER ONE

Toby slammed the door shut. He would have stamped his foot if there had been anywhere to stamp it. But that was part of the problem. His bedroom floor was knee-deep in clutter. Simply to get to the bed, he practically had to *wade* through games, models, books, and hundreds of other bits and pieces.

And he'd been told to clear the whole lot up.

"No more excuses!" said Mum. "I don't even want to see your face again, unless you're carrying some of that stuff out of your room."

She meant it, too. Toby could tell.

He picked his way across the room to the safe-

1

ty of his bed. It took real skill to know where to put down a foot and not squash something, or snap something else. This wasn't simple mess, like Sophie Hunter's bedroom. Her room was a pit. Disgusting! Crisp packets, toffee wrappers, dirty socks – and *worse*. Toby didn't even want to think about Sophie Hunter's bedroom.

No, Toby's was different. Everything jammed in his cupboards or on his shelves, or spread out on his floor, was something he'd wanted. Something he'd found or bought or swapped. Something he'd brought home proudly and been glad to have. There was no rubbish in here. And that was why he'd been sent to clear it out by himself. Mum had offered several times before.

"I'll do it for you happily," she'd said. "But I must be allowed to throw some things out."

Throw some things out? No way! Toby needed absolutely everything. Well, maybe *needed* wasn't the right word.

Wanted.

He'd wanted everything. Rolling onto his stomach across the duvet, he took a long hard look around the room. Catching sight of one or two things, it was difficult to remember why he'd wanted them so much. That Rubik cube, for example. Nobody played with them any more. But any craze can come back. You never know . . .

He'd really prefer to keep it, just in case.

How about the Beanos? Surely they could go.

But he might get ill one day, and need something good to read.

What about the games? He'd grown out of most of them, or played them so often he felt he'd never want to play them again.

But he might not be so fed up with them in a few weeks.

The snorkel? No. He might find the ping-pong ball, and manage to get it back inside the tube. The cardboard skeleton? No. Henry had hung from the curtain rail so long he was practically a friend. Surely the plastic vampire's teeth could go?

Oh no they couldn't. It was nearly Hallowe'en.

It was no good. Toby despaired. Everything he'd owned since he was practically a baby was somewhere in this room. His belongings all but flowed up the walls, but there wasn't a single thing that he felt like shoving in a bag and carrying out to the bin, or stacking in a box and taking down to the charity shop.

It was beginning to look as if Toby's mum would never see her dear son's face again.

Toby wriggled to the edge of the bed, and leaned over. Perhaps there was something hidden underneath that he could toss to the winds. The sled? Certainly not. He used that. The wellies? No, they still fitted. Mum would fly out of her cage if he threw those away. And he couldn't throw out his foreign coins or his swimming goggles or his dress-ups. He wore the bat cloak every Hallowe'en, and he needed the baggy

4

trousers to dress up as a pirate whenever his school had a Fun Day.

Wait a minute! What was this, down at the bottom of the box? Of course. It was the rusty old lamp Sophie gave him last year, in case he decided he wanted to be Aladdin for a change. But Toby much preferred pirates. So he could carry the lamp round next door and give it back to Sophie. At least then his mum would get the

5

chance to remember what he looked like!

Toby reached under the bed, and drew the old lamp out into the light. Funny. He hadn't noticed before it had such delicate tracery around the handle and up the little spout. And it was heavier than he remembered. Perhaps it was made of real brass.

Toby gave it a rub.

At first, nothing happened. The dingy metal looked just as dull and rusty as before.

Toby rubbed harder.

"Abracadabra!" he muttered to himself, without thinking. "Abracadabra!" He was so taken up with his rubbing that he didn't notice a long golden fingernail creeping silently over his shoulder.

"Abracadabra!" crooned Toby. "Abracadabra!"

A sudden glow of gold was filling the room. The air warmed, wafting the scent of flowers over his head, and there was a ripple of birdsong.

He still didn't notice. He just kept on rubbing.

"Abracadabra!" he sang merrily. "Abracadabra!"

The long golden fingernail poked Toby hard.

Dropping the lamp in fright, Toby spun round.

A genie, clothed in gold, was standing there watching him through narrowed eyes. The finger

6

that had poked Toby's shoulder was still stretched out threateningly towards him. The golden nail glittered and the genie's eyes flashed.

"Stones of the desert have sharper ears than my master!"

Now, even through his terror, Toby heard the

birdsong and smelled the warm scents, and noticed the golden glow flooding his bedroom.

He couldn't speak. He was too astonished. And far too scared to think of anything to say.

It didn't matter. The genie obviously had a lot to get off his golden chest.

"Any fool knows that it is easier to build two palaces than keep one tidy. But never in all my thousand years have I endured a resting place so like the lair of a jackal."

Toby couldn't help it. The words popped out.

"But you came from Sophie Hunter's room! That's far worse!"

The genie's lip curled at the memory, and just for a moment a picture swam into Toby's mind of this genie standing in Sophie's room amongst all the crumpled chocolate wrappers, the mugs of cold tea with fungus growing on the top – and *worse*. It was a strange vision, because everything about this genie looked so golden and perfect, from the coiled gold turban on his head to the curving gold slippers on his feet. And had he dipped his fingernails in gold, or was he really so magical that parts of him were not even flesh and blood, but made of the most precious metal? This genie looked so polished, so glisten-

8

ing, you'd think he'd be grateful to be safely away from the horrors of Sophie Hunter's bedroom.

But he sounded bad-tempered enough when he spoke.

"It's my opinion that I have fled from the rain, and sat down again under the waterspout."

It was a pity this was a subject on which Toby spent so much time arguing with his mother. As far back as he could remember, she had been comparing his bedroom with Sophie's. "You're really as messy as she is," Mum always said. "Her room may *look* a lot worse, but at least she sometimes flings a few things out. You never do." So now, with the genie starting in on him as well, Toby couldn't help trying to defend himself.

"It's all *clean*," he insisted. "And a lot of it is tidy. It's just that, over the years, I have collected quite a bit of stuff, and there isn't really room for it."

The genie looked scornful.

"The wise man takes care to raise his roof-beams *before* he brings home his camel."

Toby went red. All day, it seemed, he had been under attack about the state of his bedroom. He'd had enough.

"If you think it's such a big mess, you could always go back in your lamp."

Oh, no! What had he *said*? What had he *done*? The genie's eyes flashed sparks of golden fire.

"Beware, boy!" he hissed. "The blessings of an angry genie can fall as curses on his master's head!"

Toby turned his face away. He found it hard to think with those extraordinary golden eyes boring into him. Why had things gone so wrong so quickly? It couldn't be all Toby's fault. The genie was in a bad mood from the start. If all he wanted was to turn Toby's wishes into curses, why had he bothered to come out of the lamp?

Well, he probably had no choice about that. After all, Toby had rubbed it and said "Abracadabra!" And it couldn't be much of a life, spending most of your time trapped in a lamp, and the rest of it granting people's wishes. Toby would be bad-tempered, too, if he was stuck with that job. In fact, he'd hate every minute. He hated being told what to do. Look at this morning. Toby had argued with Mum for hours before she finally ordered him off to his bedroom. And even then he'd slammed the door.

No. Being a genie must be one of the world's worst jobs. Maybe Toby could help, now he was the master of the lamp.

He turned back to face the genie.

"Is there anything that I could wish for you?"

The genie stared.

"Well, twirl my turban!" he said softly between his teeth. "How the world changes as it spins!

11

You sit like a sultan with all your possessions around you; but when it comes to wishes, you are as different from Hasan's first master as is the generous dove from the greedy magpie!"

Toby tucked his legs more comfortably beneath him on the bed. Suddenly he felt a whole lot safer.

"Tell me about him," he said.

CHAPTER TWO

"My first master –" began the genie. Then he glanced round Toby's small cluttered bedroom with impatience.

"By the fat moon in the sky!" he cried. "Why should I labour to tell you an old tale when, in a flash, I could sweep you away and show you?"

Toby was thrilled.

"Sweep me away? What? On a magic carpet?"

The genie plucked at the duvet, making a scornful face. Then he upturned his palms, and drew his brittle gold fingernails slowly across its cover.

As Toby watched, the duvet grew thinner and

shrank to half its size. Patterns appeared on it –
the kind of ancient patterns Toby had seen on
oriental rugs. Under his legs, the duvet felt different now, more like a soft worn carpet than
fluffy bedding. It gave off a musty smell of age.
And just as Toby was about to change his mind
and beg the genie to stop, there was a sudden
glow of gold, a blinding *flash*! and all Toby could
feel was wind in his hair, and the carpet rippling
beneath him.

He screwed his eyes shut in terror.

Behind him, the genie shouted a warning into
the wind:

"Don't look down!"

The golden fingernails slid round Toby's waist.
Toby felt safe again. He did try not to look. But it
was such a chance, such an extraordinary
chance. How could you fly on a magic carpet and
not want to see it all?

He opened his eyes.

Above him – blue, blue sky. Around him – the
thin wisps of drifting cloud. Beneath him –

"Where on earth is that?"

"It is Arabia."

It was so beautiful. From up so high, the
desert was a sea of sand, stretching for ever and

14

ever. Here was a tiny island of palm trees. Miles away, almost out of sight, was another. And moving across the dunes between the two, like ships over waves, Toby saw a long line of camels. Oh, he was lucky to be high up here, winging his effortless way through the cool sky. Down there, the desert burned.

"They have so far to go!"

The genie shrugged.

"The camel is a marvellous beast. She can travel between watersprings for five days in summer and twenty-five in winter. She gives milk to drink. Her dung is fuel for cooking. And when her time is done, her sad owner cheers himself by eating her flesh and making a tent from her skin."

Toby was glad that Hasan couldn't see the look on his face.

"Doesn't seem much of a reward," he said. "For struggling over the desert with all someone's stuff on your back."

"Struggling!" the genie scoffed. "These people know a bird can only roost on one branch. They travel light. A tent, a rug, a sheepskin and a coffee pot! Why, when the Prophet Mohammed himself died, he left behind him only a shirt, a turban and an old patched robe, a waterskin and a palm-leaf mattress."

"Is that *all*? From a whole *life*?"

Behind him, Hasan snorted.

"If every person on earth had as many possessions as you, the world would soon crack from the strain! You will soon find the richest people in this world are not those who have the most things, but those who have the fewest wants.

16

Save your pity for your poor servant Hasan, who would trade all of his golden fingernails for one dish of cooling sherbet!"

Toby was delighted.

"Can I wish for you? *Please*?"

He couldn't see Hasan's face, but he did hear his sudden catch of breath. The genie held him more tightly.

"Is this your first command?"

"My very first!"

The genie's voice was strangely hoarse.

"So be it."

A sudden glow of gold warmed Toby's chest and chin. In Hasan's hand there was a sparkling dish of sherbet. One hand still held Toby firmly round the waist as the hand with the sherbet disappeared, and from behind came the tempting sound of Hasan's steady sucking.

The sherbet had looked delicious, and Toby was thirsty too. He was about to ask if he could wish for another, for himself, when suddenly he saw sweeping closer, miles beneath, a palace with glorious towers and gleaming walls.

The carpet flew nearer and nearer. Tiles of blue, green and gold glittered like jewels in the sunlight. The rooftops shone.

"It's beautiful!"

"In its day," said Hasan, "it was the most glorious palace in the world. Mind you, I show it to you at its very best. For many years now it has been nothing but rubble in the sand, and an old memory."

And not a happy one, either, thought Toby, from the tone of Hasan's voice. But, then again, he always sounded a little bit angry and bitter, as if even the golden glory of his dress and nails could not make up for some emptiness inside him. Toby was just wondering what could have happened to make Hasan this way, when suddenly the carpet swooped – down, down – towards the palace so fast that Toby was sure they would smash into its walls. He shut his eyes. But at the very last moment the carpet must have swirled round upon itself, because the next thing he felt was hot sand against his shoulder. The carpet had tumbled the two of them gently off outside the gates.

Toby picked himself up, and brushed off the burning grains of sand. Then he glanced up. The palace towered above them.

"Look at the rooftops! Are they solid gold?"

The genie's eyes followed his. Toby thought

19

he'd be thrilled to see again a place so beautiful, with all its glittering mosaics, its pillars of veined marble, its golden roofs.

But Hasan's face blackened with an old remembered rage.

"Better," he said darkly, "to have a handful of dry dates and be happy than own the Gate of Peacocks and be kicked in the eye by a broody camel."

Toby shrugged. What could he say or do? For

although Hasan had real golden fingernails, and magic at their tips, he was the moodiest creature.

Toby turned away, and peered through the gates into a leafy courtyard.

"Can we go in?"

Hasan rolled up the carpet and tucked it under his arm. Together they walked in. For just a second, Toby felt he'd been here before. But then he realised what was familiar was the sweet flowery scents Hasan brought with him when he first appeared, and the ripple of birdsong.

Hasan sat on the edge of a stone pool, and looked around sadly. Then he spread out his hands. His golden fingernails glittered in the harsh sunlight.

"This is where my story begins. Once, I was happy here . . ."

CHAPTER THREE

"Once," said Hasan, "I was happy here. I came to the palace gates as a young man, hungry and dusty. But I was quick-witted and honest. And since I was from a poor family, I knew the meaning of hard work. I could count coins faster than a hawk can drop, and so the old sultan put me in his treasury, and there I stayed until the day he died."

"And then?"

The first real smile crossed Hasan's face.

"And then the new sultan made me grand vizier."

"Grand vizier!" Toby was astonished. "But

surely that's the most important job!"

"It is indeed. I was chosen for my skills in the treasury. Under my hand, sacks of gold overflowed, and coffers bulged, and for the first time in a hundred years the counting house was as busy as an ant-heap."

"You must have been very proud."

"Proud and happy."

Hasan fell silent. Toby twisted a leaf off the branch of an orange tree behind them. He sat

quietly beside Hasan on the stone ledge of the pool, shredding the leaf to its spine. It was hard to imagine Hasan being happy. He was so – difficult to find a word for it. Hard? No, not *hard*, exactly, because Toby had the feeling there might be quite a warm-blooded person behind those harsh golden stares and sharp flashes of temper. No, it was more as if what softness there was in Hasan was trapped under his golden surface, like water rippling under a crust of ice. But he had been happy here . . .

"Things must have been very different."

"Different!" Hasan's voice was bitter. "The smiles shone from my face. I loved to hear the echo of my own footsteps ringing against the palace walls. I loved to hear the coins in my counting house, tinkling all day like the water from a fountain. But most of all I loved the new young sultan, and I blessed him each morning for giving me my chance to rise in the world – on one condition . . ."

"On one condition? What was that?"

"That I never dare to give him a word of advice about anything in the world that could neither be bought nor sold."

"But almost anything can be bought or sold."

Hasan nodded.

"And I could give advice on almost anything. I could tell him what to do with his coins and his riches. I could warn him, 'Sell that slave,' or urge him, 'Buy this one.' I could advise him about carpets and robes, horses and land, feasts and jewels. I had great power and influence. But

I would lose it all the day I dared to give a word of advice about anything in the land that could neither be bought nor sold."

"I wouldn't have risked it," said Toby after a moment's thought. "Not with a kingdom to run. It would be far too dangerous. You couldn't advise him about any of the really important things, like friends – if they could be trusted. Or war – whether to start one or stop one. Or – "

Hasan's golden eyes flashed.

"You have more wits than I, boy! I never dreamed that trouble would grow underfoot. The only worry I had was whether sacks could be sewn as fast as coins rushed in to fill them. Until the sultan fell in love . . . "

"Love!"

Toby hadn't even thought of that one. You certainly couldn't buy or sell love.

"Her name was Zubaida," said Hasan. "We called her Little Butterpat."

"Why? Was she plump?"

The genie sighed with the pleasure of the memory.

"Oh, she was better than plump! She was as round as the full moon. Once, in the counting house, I put three bulging sacks of gold onto one pan of the scales, and the sultan lifted Little Butterpat onto the other. And her pan floated down."

"It sounds to me as if she was a little bit heavier than plump."

"Yes," cried Hasan. "Why hide the truth about her beauty? Zubaida was not plump. No! She was gloriously, gloriously tubby!"

Toby couldn't help grinning.

"It also sounds to me," he said, "as if you wouldn't have given the sultan very good advice about love in any case. It sounds as if you were a

bit soft on her yourself."

Almost before the words were out of Toby's mouth, the genie's metallic eyes were glittering.

"Be quite clear, little master, I was not 'a bit soft' on Little Butterpat. I kissed the stones on which her silver slippers trod! I sent slaves to sprinkle rosewater wherever she might walk! I sent for the finest songbirds and hung their cages underneath her windows! And each time I went past a butterpat stall in the market-place, I all but fainted with joy!"

Toby took very great care to keep his face straight, and Hasan explained gravely:

"My happiness hung on hers, you see. If Little Butterpat was happy, then so was I."

"And was she?"

"Oh, she was happy as a lark. So was the sultan. Each morning, when he woke, he said to her: 'Bite my finger, beloved, so I may know if this happiness I feel is a dream!' "

"And did she?"

"Did she what?"

"Bite his finger each morning."

The genie stared, then asked irritably:

"Boy! Have you never *loved*?"

Toby gave it a moment's reflection. He'd had a

bit of a crush on Miss Adulewebe for a while, till she told him off twice in a row for doing sloppy work. And Mum often joked about the way he chased Sophie Hunter round the nursery playground, trying to kiss her. But he was only four then.

He was a lot older now. And he certainly wouldn't fancy having his finger bitten every morning.

"No, never," he said firmly. "I've never been in love."

"Then you won't understand," declared Hasan. "You won't know the joy of standing in a courtyard at night watching the one you worship counting the stars! Hearing her guess the words that the songbird you gave her is singing! Listening to her tell her fortune in the dregs of her sherbet!"

Oh, really! thought Toby. Op, plop. Pass the mop! But just at that moment a golden tear began to roll down Hasan's cheek.

"Oh!" he wailed. "I was so happy, here at the fountain beside my master and his beloved, listening to the nightingale!"

In silence Toby waited for the tear to fall with a splash on the hot stones between Hasan's slippers. But:

Ping!

He couldn't have imagined it! The tear was actually rolling away!

"Is that tear made of *real gold*?"

Hasan looked wretched.

"Permit me to weep you a bucketful," he offered.

Toby was horrified.

"No. Please don't! No."

Hasan looked more than ready. On each lower lid, tiny gold tears were welling.

Toby was desperate to distract him.

"I wish – " he cried. (For surely, if Hasan had

work to do, he wouldn't have time to cry.)

"I wish – "

The twin tears trembled. Hasan looked so miserable that Toby could only think of one thing to wish.

"I wish you could be with the sultan and Zubaida again, hearing the nightingale's best song!"

There it was a second time – that little catch of breath. The genie gripped Toby by the elbows

and looked half-mad with hope.

"Is it your second wish?"

For just a moment, Toby hesitated. After all, he didn't know how many wishes he was going to get. It might be only three. He'd already used one up getting Hasan that sherbet. Now he was about to spend another trying to cheer him up.

But what else could he do?

"Yes, it's my second wish."

There was a sudden glow of gold. A brilliant *flash*! And before he knew what had hit him, or how, poor Toby was tumbling – back, back, back, backwards through the hot and scented air, into the water of the pool.

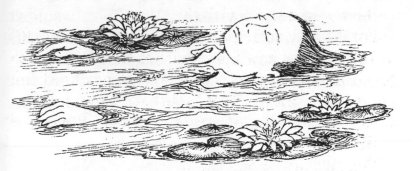

CHAPTER FOUR

Oh, bliss! Oh, heaven! Oh, perfect joy! He hadn't realised quite how hot he was, till he fell into the water. It filled his ears, blotting out everything but tendrils of weed and the spangles of sunlight above him. There was no room to swim. The pool was little more than a stone tank, not very much deeper than a bath. But Toby could stretch himself out – now floating – now letting himself sink – now using a fingertip to push himself up again. His hair fanned around his face like more dark weed. He was perfectly, perfectly happy.

And so, it seemed, was Hasan. Each time Toby floated up to break the surface and take a lungful of air, he could hear the song of a bird, and snatches of happy chatter. But Toby wouldn't look. What was the point of giving Hasan his wish, and then spoiling it by being nosy? He'd love to peep at Little Butterpat and the sultan. But Hasan wasn't daft. Toby hadn't fetched up under-water by accident. Hasan had tipped him in. It

must be for a reason. Perhaps the moment Toby lifted his head clear of the water to take a look at Hasan's friends, the nightingale would stop singing and the two of them would vanish.

Give him time. Give him time . . .

Did minutes pass? Or hours? Toby lost track. When the gold fingernail dipped in to prod him, all Toby knew was that he'd been left to wallow in the cool water of the stone tank the perfect length of time. No more, no less.

Hasan pulled him out, then stepped back as puddles of water spread from Toby's shoes, threatening his own golden slippers.

"How was the water, little master?"

Toby shook his fringe like a dog, splattering drops all round.

"Perfect," he said. "How did the wish go?"

The genie did try to answer. But Toby could see he couldn't find the words. After a moment he gave up the struggle and, slipping an arm around Toby, said to him instead:

"A walk around the palace, while you dry!"

Together they strolled through the courtyard. First Hasan pushed open the door to the counting house.

"No need to step inside. You can see all you

need from here."

But Toby was curious. After all, this was where Hasan had spent years of his life. Before the genie could stop him, he'd slipped through the door, and taken a good look around. The tables were heaped high with coins, as if Hasan had left off counting only yesterday. Great piles of sacks blocked most of the tiny windows. But in the corner Toby suddenly saw two strange golden statues, lit by a dusty shaft of light. They were taller than Toby, and dressed in the finest robes. Could they be statues of the sultan and Zubaida?

The woman was certainly – what was it? – as round as the full moon. But the man was staring at the woman in shock, and the woman was pointing in anger. That couldn't be right. The sultan and Little Butterpat were supposed to be happy as a dream.

"Who are – "

But Hasan had stepped in after him, and gripping Toby firmly by the arm, hurried him out again.

"Come. There is much more to see."

Much, much more. Toby never forgot the way his eyes were dazzled as the genie led him through one glittering chamber after another, each stuffed with more treasures than the last. At first Toby ran everywhere, trying to touch everything he saw. Later he walked more slowly, and only bothered to stretch out a hand to pat the ivory saddle of this rocking horse, or lift a jewelled piece from that chess board. And by the time Hasan had led him all the way round the palace and back to where they began, Toby was stifling a yawn.

"So much *stuff*!"

Behind, through the door of the counting house, Toby heard a little sob. But in there stood only the two golden statues. He would have thought that he'd imagined it, but when he turned back he was just in time to see the look of pain crossing Hasan's face.

"Did you hear someone sobbing?"

Hasan's face went stony.

"No one is there, little master."

"But I heard someone sobbing. So did you."

Stubbornly, Hasan repeated:

"No one is there. It is the echo of a memory."

But Toby had already guessed. What else could cause Hasan so much pain?

"It's Little Butterpat, isn't it? She was crying! But why? I thought the three of you were supposed to be so happy!"

A hunted look came over Hasan's face. He waved his hands about vaguely.

"No one is happy all the time. Even the heart may have a summer and a winter."

But Toby wasn't satisfied with that.

"Did the sultan stop loving her? Was that it?"

It seemed to Toby that Hasan was torn between saying nothing and defending his old friend. In the end, loyalty won.

"No, no. He loved her always. But as the years passed, he let himself care about his treasures more and more. 'Come and walk with me,' she would say to him. And he would reply: 'Soon, soon.' 'Come and talk to me.' 'Soon, soon.' And Little Butterpat would wander through the

palace, lonely and bored, while the sultan spent his time with his riches."

Without thinking, Toby burst out:

"You should have warned him! You should have given him a word of advice!"

Then he saw Hasan's face, and remembered.
Hasan buried his head in his hands.
"I was a fool!" he cried. "I should have spoken!

40

What did it matter that I would lose everything and find myself outside the palace gates again, dusty and hungry! A man has no more goods than he gets good by. And the love of Little Butterpat – because it was a thing that could neither be bought nor sold – was worth more than all the treasures in the palace!"

Toby tried to comfort him.

"But the sultan was to blame too!"

Hasan lifted his head from his hands.

"Oh, yes. Blame the sultan too! For Little Butterpat came to the door of the counting house a thousand times. 'Come and dance with me.' 'Come and sing with me.' But the sultan only answered: 'Soon, soon.' And I – I cared more for all I had gained than for all I would lose, and said nothing – nothing at all!"

Hasan broke off, sobbing himself now.

Ping! Ping! Ping! Ping!

The golden tears rained down.

Hoping to comfort him, Toby moved closer and slipped an arm round his shoulder. To his astonishment, it felt brittle to his touch, and he couldn't help stepping back, startled.

Hasan lifted a face with gold tears rolling down but not a tearstain in sight.

Ping! Ping! Ping! Ping!

"See!" he cried. "Even my golden tears mock me! If Little Butterpat could only see the curse she put on me, her tears would flow as freely as mine do now!"

Ping! Ping! Ping! Ping!

Toby was horrified.

"She put a *curse* on you? What? Out of *spite*?"

The genie shook his head. Tears scattered far and wide.

Ping! Ping! Ping! Ping!

Taking a deep breath, Toby slid his arm around the genie's shoulders, and squeezed him as hard as he dare. Gradually, the pinging slowed.

Ping! Ping!

"Tell me what happened. Please. Finish the story."

Ping!

Kicking his last tear away, Hasan took up his tale.

CHAPTER FIVE

"Some days," said Hasan, "winds cut across the desert like hot knives. Dogs snapped and babies cried. Everyone stood at the door of ill-temper. And on one of those days, Zubaida came here, to the counting house."

Hasan stepped inside. Toby followed. Hasan pointed to some coin sacks in the corner.

"We had just counted those. The sultan was sitting watching us fill yet another sack, when in she walked."

"Come and dance with me!" murmured Toby. "Come and sing with me!"

The genie smiled. "And the sultan replied:

'Soon, soon.'"

"Everything the same as usual," said Toby.

"Not quite. For the hot winds had caught at Little Butterpat and sharpened her temper and nerves. 'Who could need all this gold?' she demanded of the sultan. 'All is not gain that is put in the purse. Your treasures are bought too dear. You have become a slave to your possessions. Even the richest man can carry nothing but his shroud away with him. So give your riches to those who will use them. He who learns giving as well as getting has no need for a counting house at all!'

"Then she turned and held her hands out to me.

" 'Tell him, grand vizier!'she begged me."

Toby bit his lip. He could see that the genie was still ashamed of the memory.

"And I said nothing – not a word of advice."

"What happened?"

Hasan sighed. "Oh, it was not a day for lovers! The sultan was piqued. 'What do you know about these things?' he asked Little Butterpat scornfully. 'You who would spend your days dancing and talking, laughing and singing! What do you know about the value of things that can be bought and sold?'

"Now her eyes flashed.

"'More than you think,' she told him haughti-ly. 'I know the value of all the riches in this counting house!'

"The sultan's voice took on the edge of steel.

"'What's this?' he said. 'Can you see through the weave of a sack, and count the coins inside?' And he reached down to where, at his feet, lay a lamp so dull and rusty that no one had bothered

to lift it from the floor. Holding it high, he cried out to all who would listen:

" 'Here is a prize for Little Butterpat, if she can tell me the value of all the riches in my counting house!' "

Toby felt his stomach knotting.

"It was a day fit only for dogs," said Hasan. "Drawing herself up, Zubaida replied with all the scorn of one who has spent too many days wandering alone through a palace:

" 'Your riches are worth nothing!' "

Now Toby could see the sultan in Hasan's face, and hear him in his voice.

" 'Nothing?' "

" 'Nothing!' "

" 'How so, my beloved?' he asked, dangerous as a cobra.

" 'Because,' she cried, 'your riches are like camel dung! No use to anyone till they are spread!'

" 'Camel dung!' shouted the sultan. Oh, it was a day for scorpions! And in his fury, he flung the lamp."

"Did it hit her?"

"It tangled in the folds of her robes. And as she reached to shake it off with one hand, she pointed at the sultan with the other.

46

"'Gold! Gold!' she cried. 'I wish you were turned to gold. And since you love gold more than the living, I wish I were turned to gold too!' Her fingers brushed the lamp, which suddenly started to glow. 'Stop!' cried the sultan. 'It is a magic lamp. Take back your wish, and quickly!' But she did not hear because in her anger she had turned to me.

"'As for you, grand vizier, I wish you were

imprisoned forever in this old lamp, cursed with a body turning day by day to gold, and forced to serve one greedy, grasping master after another until –'"

Hasan broke off.

"Until *what*?" Toby demanded. "Until *what*?"

Hasan shook his head.

"I may not say. And barely were the words out of her mouth before she was turned to gold, and the sultan too, and I – "

But Toby had shut his eyes and clapped his hands over his ears.

"Don't tell me any more! I can't stand it! It's too awful. Oh, how I wish the three of you could go back in time and start that day again!"

Now there it was, for the third time, that sudden catch of breath. Toby opened his eyes. Hasan was staring at him with a wild look of hope.

"Is that your third and last wish?"

Last? Oh, no! Only three wishes! He'd spent the first on a dish of sherbet, the second on a song, and now the third was going! How could things have worked out this way? But, then again, thought Toby. What would he wish for if he had more time to think? Only more stuff to clutter up his bedroom. And if he had learned

48

anything at all from Hasan, it was that the things that could not be bought or sold were more valuable than anything else.

So let the wish go if it made Hasan happy.

"Yes! Yes! It's my third and last wish!"

The sudden glow of gold that lit the counting house was richer than any before. The air filled with soft scents and the glorious ripple of birdsong. And Hasan stood, taller than before, repeating softly under his breath the last words of Zubaida's wish.

" – cursed to serve one greedy, grasping master after another until you find one whose wishes are all for another, not for himself."

Now it was Toby's turn to stare.

"I've done it! Haven't I?"

The genie pressed his hands together, and bowed low.

"I had no hopes," he said. "I saw your room, crammed full of everything you ever owned, and my heart sank. But you have done it."

He had, too. Already shreds of gold were falling from Hasan, showering to the floor. His fingernails were peeling. The harsh gold of his eyes was changing back to soft brown, and from them tears were spilling onto the stones.

Splash! Splash! Splash! Splash!

Real tears! Hasan was weeping tears of joy, for before his very eyes the two golden statues were coming back to life, reaching for one another and smiling. The dreadful, dreadful day was starting all over again, but this time it would be different, and so would the future.

Then suddenly Hasan came to his senses.

"Quick!" he cried, brushing away his tears. "Hurry, before the glow fades and you are stuck forever out of time!"

Unfurling the carpet, he pushed Toby down flat.

"Shut your eyes! Hold tightly!"

He gave Toby no choice. Before the glow of gold could fade away entirely, the carpet rose. Rippling steadily, it flew up – up, up – high in the sky and away, and once again Toby could feel cool breezes lifting his hair.

He lay flat, as he'd been told, holding on tightly. Beneath him the carpet was soft. Indeed, the further it flew, the softer it felt, more like a duvet lulling Toby into drowsiness. When he got home again, he'd clear out his cupboards, give a lot of things away. What was the point of hanging on to everything? He didn't want to be a slave to his possessions. After all, even the richest man can carry nothing but his shroud away with him. And riches were only like camel dung really - not much use till they were spread.

He'd take the games and models and some of the other stuff he hardly ever used down to the charity shop on the corner. And he could give Sophie the comics. As soon as he got home he'd stack the whole lot in boxes and carry them out of his room.

That way Mum would get to see her dear son's face again . . .

That would be good . . .

Before the journey even ended, Toby was asleep.